FARM ANIMALS

Pigs

by Emily K. Green

SKOKIE PUBLIC LIBRARY

BLASTOFF! READERS

BELLWETHER MEDIA • MINNEAPOLIS, MN

Note to Librarians, Teachers, and Parents:

Blastoff! Readers are carefully developed by literacy experts and combine standards-based content with developmentally appropriate text.

Level 1 provides the most support through repetition of high-frequency words, light text, predictable sentence patterns, and strong visual support.

Level 2 offers early readers a bit more challenge through varied simple sentences, increased text load, and less repetition of high-frequency words.

Level 3 advances early-fluent readers toward fluency through increased text and concept load, less reliance on visuals, longer sentences, and more literary language.

Whichever book is right for your reader, Blastoff! Readers are the perfect books to build confidence and encourage a love of reading that will last a lifetime!

This edition first published in 2007 by Bellwether Media.

No part of this publication may be reproduced in whole or in part without written permission of the publisher. For information regarding permission, write to Bellwether Media Inc., Attention: Permissions Department, Post Office Box 1C, Minnetonka, MN 55345-9998.

Library of Congress Cataloging-in-Publication Data
Green, Emily K., 1966–
  Pigs / by Emily K. Green.
    p. cm. – (Blastoff! readers. Farm animals)
Summary: "A basic introduction to pigs and how they live on the farm. Simple text and full color photographs. Developed by literacy experts for students in kindergarten through third grade"–Provided by publisher.
 Includes bibliographical references and index.
 ISBN-13: 978-1-60014-068-6 (hardcover : alk. paper)
 ISBN-10: 1-60014-068-8 (hardcover : alk. paper)
 1. Swine–Juvenile literature. I. Title.

SF395.5.G74 2007
636.4–dc22   2006035308

Text copyright © 2007 by Bellwether Media.
SCHOLASTIC, CHILDREN'S PRESS, and associated logos are trademarks and/or registered trademarks of Scholastic Inc.
Printed in the United States of America.

Contents

Pigs on a Farm	4
Parts of a Pig	8
What Pigs Eat	12
Pigs Keep Cool	18
Glossary	22
To Learn More	23
Index	24

Pigs can live on a farm.

A **sow** is
a mother pig.
A **piglet** is
a young pig.

Pigs have a short, curly tail.

Pigs have a flat nose called a **snout**.

Pigs eat many things. They can eat plants or meat. Farmers can also buy special pig food.

Some pigs are pink. Pigs can be other colors too.

Short, stiff hair covers a pig's body.

A pig can get a **sunburn** just like you can. Pigs need shade on sunny days.

Pigs roll in the mud to keep cool. Aaaahhh!

Glossary

piglet—a baby pig

snout—the long, flat nose of a pig; pigs use their noses to dig for roots in the ground.

sow—an adult female pig

sunburn—sore, red skin that happens after you have been in the sun for too long

To Learn More

AT THE LIBRARY

Dicamillo, Kate. *Mercy Watson to the Rescue*. Cambridge, Mass.: Candlewick Press, 2005.

Lobel, Arnold. *Small Pig*. New York: Harper & Row, 1969.

Palatini, Margie. *Oink*? New York: Simon & Schuster, 2006.

Walton, Rick. *Pig, Pigger, Piggest*. Layton, Utah: Gibbs Smith, 2003.

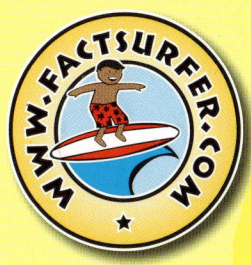

ON THE WEB

Learning more about farm animals is as easy as 1, 2, 3.

1. Go to www.factsurfer.com

2. Enter "farm animals" into search box.

3. Click the "Surf" button and you will see a list of related web sites.

With factsurfer.com, finding more information is just a click away.

Index

body, 16
colors, 14
farm, 4
farmers, 12
food, 12
hair, 16
meat, 12
mother, 6
mud, 20
nose, 10
piglet, 6
pink, 14
plants, 12
shade, 18

snout, 10
sow, 6
sunburn, 18
tail, 8

The photographs in this book are reproduced through the courtesy of: Bill Ling/Getty Images, front cover; Mark Moffet/Getty Images, p. 5; tadija, p. 7; Peter Dean/Alamy, p. 9; Thorsten Milse/Getty Images, p. 11; Peter Cade/Getty Images, p. 13; Kay Ransom, p. 15; Shawn Hine, p. 17; Chris Mercer/Alamy, p. 19; John Peters, p. 21.